One Heart

Written by: Tara Drouin

Illustrated by: Nancy Noskewicz

Thankyou for buying One Heart! I hope you love the illustrations ☺ Love, Ms.N

Dedicated to Kaya

MW01094836

Our skin might be a different shade.

Our hair can be straight or curly.

Our eyes can be

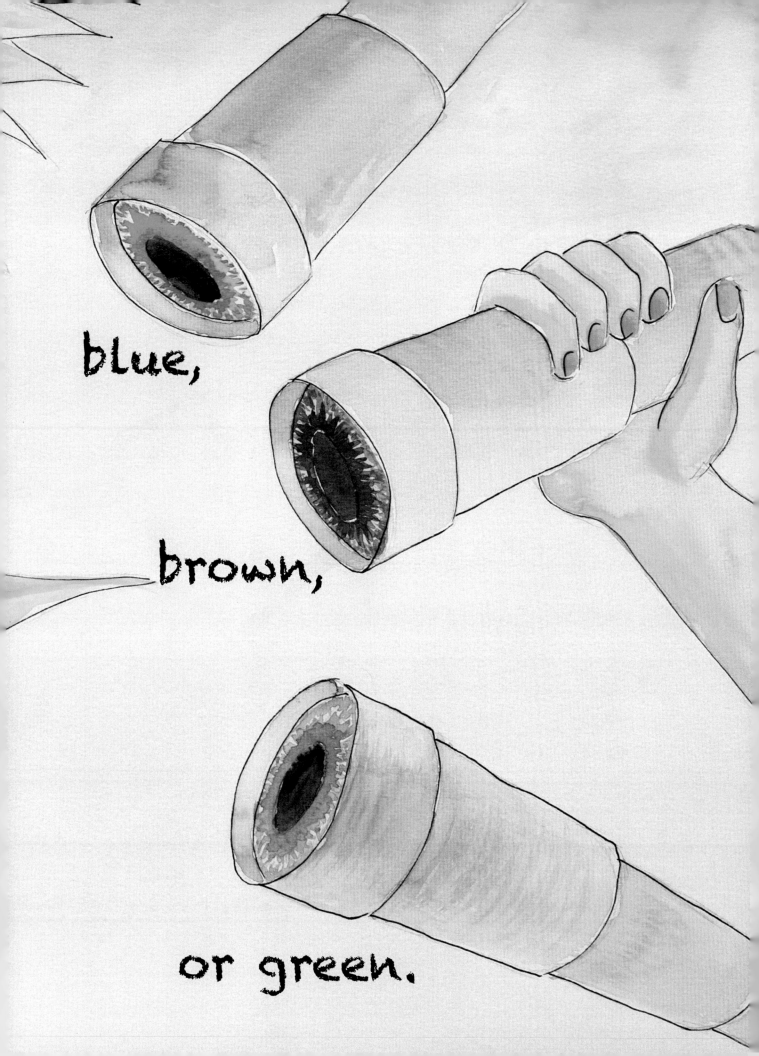

blue,

brown,

or green.

Inside everybody's got one heart.

When you wake up,

each day's a brand new start.

Because inside everybody's got one heart.

We may not all feel the same. He likes the sun,

she likes the rain.

He gets up late.

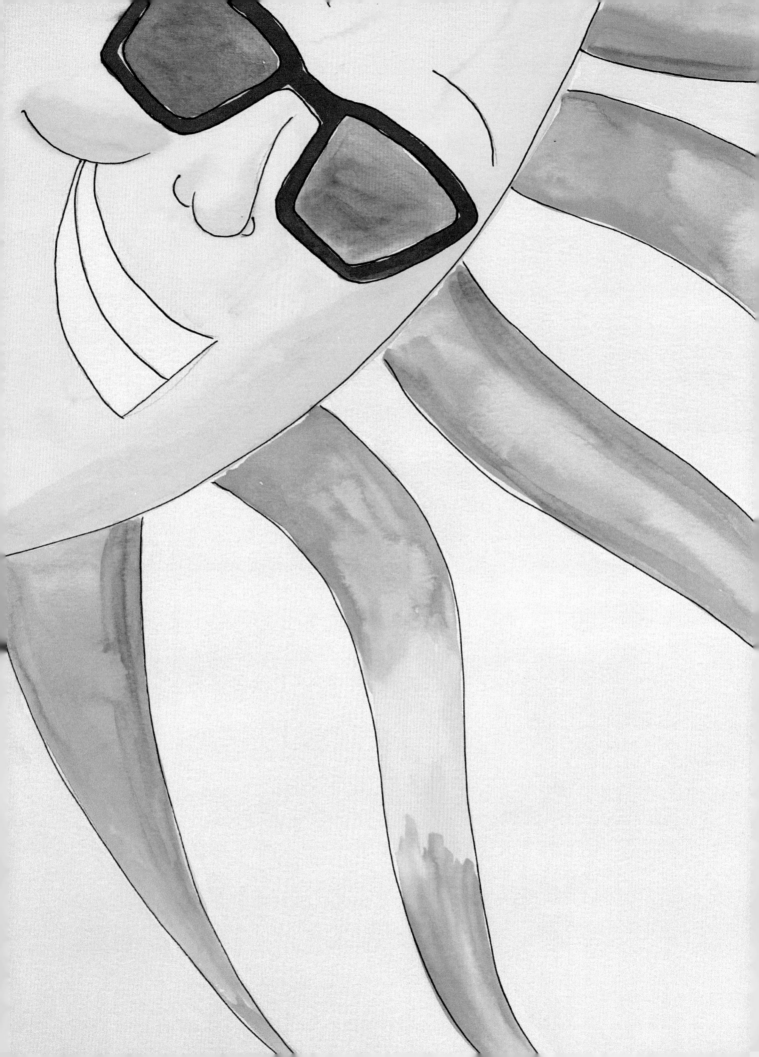

She gets up early.

We like to learn about new things. Especially learning to sing.

Voices come together, there's nothing better.

Inside everybody's got one heart.

When you wake up,

each day's a brand new start.

Because inside everybody's got one heart.

And if you want to make things happen.

you want to live in a better world.

Recreate the love and unity.

Time's about to start and stop.

And when you look inside,
you got love, for everyone.

Inside everybody's got one heart.
When you wake up,
each day's a brand new start.

Because inside everybody's got

one heart.

75660642R00020

Made in the USA
Middletown, DE
07 June 2018